Standing on Custard

Children's books

www.standingoncustard.com

'Standing on Custard' and **'A Squirrel's Tail'** are written by Jo Burke. "I wanted to create classic children's books full of love, wit, charm and memorable characters that bring a smile to your face."

Jo is an author, actor and comedian. Her debut book **'iScream'** reached N° 17 on Amazon. She wrote, produced and performed six, four star, Edinburgh Festival shows between 2010-2015 and was a "So You Think That's Funny?" Finalist in 2015.

Phillip Price illustrates Jo's work using watercolour. He is an artist, photographer and teacher. He has been published by Hodder Education and Zig-Zag Publications for a number of educational resources.

Thank you for supporting independent publishing. Please spread the word, leave a review and follow or like *Standing on Custard* on FaceBook, Instagram and Twitter.

CW00867676

First published in the UK August 2017 by EZE Publications.

Copyright © Jo Burke 2017

Illustrations copyright © Phillip Price & Jo Burke 2017

All rights reserved. No part of this publication may be reproduced, stored in a retrieval system or transmitted in any form or by any means, electronic, mechanical, photocopying, recording or otherwise without the permission of the author and illustrator.

ISBN 978-0-9576250-3-7

Age 3+

A Squirrel's Tail

To Jack

Enjoy!

Written by Jo Burke

Illustrated by Phillip Price

Jo Burke (signature)

Sheridan Squirrel was no ordinary squirrel.

He was very, very, **very** special.

What was so special about Sheridan Squirrel?

Sheridan Squirrel was born extra small and without a tail.

At first Sheridan was sad he had no tail. In fact he tried many, many,

many replacements.

Sheridan tried... a hair brush instead of a tail...

... duck feathers instead of a tail...

...he even tried to make a new tail from a leaf!

Sheridan wanted to be the same as all the other squirrels and have a long, bushy tail. Some of the mean squirrels laughed at him. They called him names like "Bunny" and "Stumpy."

You see, the most squirrelly thing about a squirrel is, of course, its tail. They need their tails to keep warm and for balance so they can leap from tree to tree and from branch to branch.

Without a tail Sheridan found it hard to do squirrelly things. He couldn't jump from tree to tree like his friends. He tried and tried. He would take a big deep breath and a long run up and go splat! Straight into the side of the tree.

He was always cold too as he had no tail to wrap around him. So his dad knitted him a smart cardigan. Sheridan loved his bright red, homemade cardigan. He was the only squirrel with a cardigan and it made him feel extra special and as warm as toast.

One day, an old, retired, racing pigeon with one claw, called Paloma said, "Sheridan I think you run faster and are smarter than any squirrel I've ever met."

"Really?" asked Sheridan whilst Paloma bandaged his sore head.

"Yes," said Paloma, "although I've no idea why you run head first into trees. Have you tried going around them?"

In bed that night Sheridan thought about what Paloma had said. He **was** fast and clever. What if, instead of trying to do what all the other squirrels do, he did something else?

Slowly Sheridan dozed off under his bedcovers made of leaves. He dreamt of winning Gold in the next Squirrel Paralympics for the 100 metres sprint.

The next day Sheridan admitted to Paloma, "I'm so tired of trying to be like everyone else."

"Oh Sheridan, never try to be like other squirrels. Just be the best you. That's something no one else can do," Paloma cooed as she stroked his head.

"Be the best me? How?" sniffed Sheridan.

"It's easier than you think. Simply focus on what you are good at, do what you enjoy and **always** follow your heart."

"You're shivering. Are you cold?" Sheridan asked Paloma.

"I'm not shivering. I've got an itchy back do you think you could scratch it for me?" Paloma had a plan.

"I can't reach."

"Climb up on my wing."

Sheridan climbed up Paloma's wing and onto her back.

"Hold on tight," squawked Paloma with delight as she flew up, up, up into the air.

"Woohoo, woowoah," Sheridan squealed.

"Prepare for landing," shouted Paloma over the wind.

"Wooowhhhhaaaatttttt? - Phew!" Sheridan's heart was beating so fast he could hardly breathe. "I'm at the top of the tree," gasped Sheridan.

"Which tree would you like to fly to now?"

"The tallest tree in the park please!" Sheridan smiled from ear to ear.

Just then, two of the meanest squirrels spotted Sheridan. "Oi! Stumpy Bunny. How did you get up here?"

"With a little help from a friend," said Paloma preening herself proudly.

"Who asked you Wonky Pigeon?"

With that, as quick as a flash, Paloma gave Sheridan two of her feathers and he sprinted over to the meanies holding the feathers aloft. Then he did a little dance and tickled them until they fell off the branch helpless with laughter.

"Do you think they'll be okay?" Paloma said, only mildly concerned.

"Yes of course. They've got tails and can fly from branch to branch. So they won't fall."

"Whenever you want to fly I can be your tail. Hop on board and we can go wherever you want."

"Really? I can go further and higher than any squirrel has ever gone before? Oh thank you," said Sheridan as he hugged Paloma.

That night Sheridan told his dad he'd flown to the top of a tree on Paloma's back. He could tell his dad didn't believe him. But he knew he'd been there and it wouldn't be the last time he flew. Sheridan and Paloma were a team now.

He would have to invent a way that they could hear each other over the wind. He had an idea. He started working on it under the bedcovers by the light of Freddie the Firefly.

"Are they bottle tops?" yawned Paloma the next morning.

"Exactly right," said Sheridan. "Do you know what they are for?"

"Hmm now let me guess. Keeping drinks fresh?"

"That's what they **were** for. What they're for **now** is entirely different.

I present to you, Paloma Pigeon, my new in-flight hearing invention.

These will mean we can hear each other when we're flying."

Sheridan popped two bottle tops connected with a paper clip over her head and positioned the other cap, connected by a cotton bud, beside her beak.

Once on board he placed the other set on his own head. Their two bottle top headsets were connected with pieces of string.

"CAN YOU HEAR ME, PALOMA?" He shouted.

"LOUD AND CLEAR, CAPTAIN SHERIDAN."

"Who needs a tail anyway!" Sheridan proudly exclaimed.

"Let the adventures begin," Paloma cooed as she took flight.

Off they flew. Higher and higher. Faster and faster. Whilst all the other squirrels, including the meanies and his dad, looked up in utter amazement.

As they swooped overhead Sheridan waved and shouted to his dad...

"Look Dad. I **can** fly!"

Quick Quiz

1) What three things does Sheridan try to use as a tail?

2) What does Paloma have missing?

3) What does Sheridan use to tickle the mean squirrels?

4) What colour medal does Sheridan dream of winning?

5) What type of tree does Paloma take him to the top of?

6) What colour is Sherdian's cardigan?

7) Name one of the things Sheridan uses so he can hear Paloma?

Good luck!

You can download 'A Squirrel's Tail' to your iPad or iPhone from the iBooks Store.

Also by Jo Burke:

Standing on Custard
Molly, Chip and the Chair

For more information about Jo's books or to order online go to:
www.standingoncustard.com